WORLDS APART

Traveling With Fernie and Me

Poems by **Gary Soto**

Illustrated by **Greg Clarke**

G. P. PUTNAM'S SONS   NEW YORK

G.P. PUTNAM'S SONS
A division of Penguin Young Readers Group
Published by The Penguin Group
Penguin Group (USA) Inc., 375 Hudson Street, New York, NY 10014, U.S.A.
Penguin Group (Canada), 10 Alcorn Avenue, Toronto, Ontario, Canada M4V 3B2
    (a division of Pearson Penguin Canada Inc.)
Penguin Books Ltd, 80 Strand, London WC2R ORL, England.
Penguin Ireland, 25 St. Stephen's Green, Dublin 2, Ireland (a division of Penguin Books Ltd.)
Penguin Books India Pvt Ltd, 11 Community Centre, Panchsheel Park, New Delhi - 110 017, India.
Penguin Group (NZ), Cnr Airborne and Rosedale Roads, Albany, Auckland, New Zealand
    (a division of Pearson New Zealand Ltd).
Penguin Books (South Africa) (Pty) Ltd, 24 Sturdee Avenue, Rosebank, Johannesburg 2196, South Africa.
Penguin Books Ltd, Registered Offices: 80 Strand, London WC2R ORL, England.

Published simultaneously in Canada. Printed in the United States of America.
Design by Gunta Alexander. Text set in Quorum Medium.

Library of Congress Cataloging-in-Publication Data
Soto, Gary. Worlds apart : traveling with Fernie and me : poems / by Gary Soto ; illustrated by Greg Clarke.
p. cm. Summary: Eager to see what lies beyond their own back yards, Fernie and his friend take an
imaginary trip around the world. 1. Voyages, Imaginary—Juvenile poetry. 2. Travelers—Juvenile poetry.
3. Children's poetry, American. 4. Travel—Juvenile poetry. [1. Imagination—Poetry. 2. Travel—Poetry.
3. Voyages around the world—Poetry. 4. American poetry.] I. Clarke, Greg, 1959– ill. II. Title.
PS3569.072W67 2005   811'.54—dc22   2004001888   ISBN 0-399-24218-X
10 9 8 7 6 5 4 3 2 1 First Impression

For Bobbi Fisher,
and for Laura Malagón—*siempre.* —G. S.

To Keevin P. Lewis. —G. C.

Contents

Itching to Travel

Me, I tried sightseeing from a limb in a backyard tree.
Fernie tried sitting on a car fender.
Me, I tried sailing in a bathtub with its swamp of hot water.
Fernie tried lounging in his bedroom,
A museum of dirty T-shirts and stiff socks.
Me, I tried a tour on a city bus across town.
Fernie tried vacationing on the ninth hole of an abandoned
    golf course.
Me, I tried collecting foreign coins.
Fernie tried licking used stamps and pasting them into a
    scrapbook.

We itched to go places,
To double-tie our shoes and roll away on skateboards.
And why? We knew only our back and front yards,
School and the playground,
A mall where in the plastic trees were perched plastic birds.
Their beaks were open, but what were they singing?

So one morning
Fernie and me jumped off the roof of the doghouse
And started up the street, our shadows struggling to keep up.

We figured if they got lost,
They could just follow our sunflower-seed shells
Lying in the road.

San Francisco Fog

Somewhere a boat honked.
Somewhere a seagull cleaned its beak under its arm.

Somewhere a jogger huffed past, his own breath like fog.
Somewhere a dog toppled a garbage can.

Where are you? I called to Fernie.
Come out of the fog!

The fog was thick on a Sunday morning when the church bells
Had yet to clang and shake off their pigeons.
The cold kept
People inside their houses,
Rubbing their hands together like sticks.

I took a step and absently nudged against a pigeon,
Itself the color of fog.

Excuse me, I said to the bird,
And that street bird warbled.
I tossed my little friend a handful of sunflower seeds.

I walked to a pier, or what I thought was a pier.
Silence. Just the sound of waves against rock.
Wait, I was hasty. I picked up the sound of someone licking
    his lips.
Wait, there was more! The sound of something being swallowed.

In the grayness I bumped into Fernie.

What a dude! Fernie was dunking a doughnut into hot chocolate,

Hiding in fog, I guess, because he didn't want to share!

When he said, Hey, I was looking for you,

His breath, doughnut shaped, hung in front of his face,

A sweet lie in the cold, cold air.

Luxury Liner

I said, This is nice!
Fernie agreed by wiggling his toes.
He sipped on a drink called
Pineapple Madness on the Way to Hawaii.

We rolled on the ocean,
A seagull or two following the ship.
The waves were tipped with sunlight.

Me, I ordered a Volcano,
A drink with a red syrup gurgling out of the top.
I sipped and my tongue appraised the sweetness.
I said, Boy, that's nice.

Fernie looked at me.
How nice? he asked, pushing his sunglasses onto his head.
The shadow of a seagull's wing crossed his face.
I could see that he was curious.

I passed my drink to him, and he passed his to me.

Ready? Fernie asked.
I nodded my head and heard him count one, two, three.

We sucked on each other's drink
Until our cheeks were bloated.

We wiggled our toes.

I handed back his drink, and he handed back mine.

Yours is really, really good, I said,

And Fernie wiggled a toe sideways—no, no, no.

Yours is way better.

The ship rolled over the waves.

We ordered the same thing,

But this time mixed the drinks.

We were chemists tossing a little into his glass,

A little into mine—a new flavor

We anointed Volcano Hawaii.

On such fuel we did laps among the old folks in the pool.

Waikiki Beach

In Hawaii, Fernie buried me in sand
Until all that was left were my two eyes, my two nostrils.

Fernie ran for the waves.
I stared at the sky, fell asleep,
Until an ant circled first my left nostril, then my right,
Then again my left.

When he started to climb down the dark cavern,
I sneezed and blew away the little creature.

That'll teach him, I thought of the ant,
And fell back to sleep,
A rock or two of sand falling into my nostrils
But not much.

When I woke,
A sand crab, dressed in armor, was looking at me.
Each of his eyes was like the period of a long sentence,
Small, small, small.

Oh, man, I thought, the ant has brought his big brother!

The crab clicked his claws and crossed his antennae like swords.
Me, I blinked, flared my nostrils, and crossed my eyes.

When the crab raised a snapping claw,
I twitched my mouth back and forth until my teeth,
All yellow from pounding down cheese sandwiches,
Broke through the sand.
I grinned and chattered my teeth like castanets.

The crab backed up, scared.
Now it's his turn, I thought, for him to bury himself,
Time for him to set his eyes—periods—on the sandy surface.
How he breathed through a nose, a tube, a hole
On the top of his head, I didn't know.

Australia Backwoods

Weighing in at 95 pounds, from the United States . . .
(Fernie shadowboxed under a tree,
His feet swift,
His stomach flat as cardboard flattened in the road.)

. . . of America, formerly ranked 1,003,376 in the world
And now ranked 3,349,237 . . .
Chicken Legs Fernie.

Fernie bowed to the kangaroo
Where I sat oh so comfortably in his pouch,
A stopwatch in one hand, a small bell in the other.

When I yelled, Round one!
The two fighters began to box,
Or sort of box. They moved in front of each other,
Jabbing but not hitting,
Stopping to admire each other's trunks,
Another time for Fernie to retie his shoelaces.

They boxed, these two champions of their own dreams.
They swung at each other
And missed and missed.
They stirred up a breeze in each other's face.
They grunted, they winced, they closed their eyes.

They clenched, hurting my head a little, squishing my ears,
Me, the boy in the kangaroo's pouch.
But smart me, I rang the bell.
I breathed harder than these fighters.

Round two! I yelled,
And Fernie and the kangaroo began again
By shuffling their feet, jabbing but not connecting.
They leaned against each other's shoulder.
Again, my head was slammed against Fernie's pigeon chest.

Round three, round four,
Each round no longer than sixteen seconds
Because I was the fellow taking all the knocks.

At the end of ten rounds, I climbed out of the pouch,
Dizzy but still on my staggering feet,
Me, the referee with a bell in my hand
And two others ringing in my ears.

Tattoos

In the Philippines
Fernie and me got tattoos,
Lots of them. We had them all up
And down our arms,
On our legs, down near our ankles
Where you had to bend over really far to read:
FERNIE AND ME, WORLD TRAVELERS.

I had tattoos on my fingertips,
And Fernie had some on his eyelids.
I looked inside Fernie's ear—
A tattoo read, LISTEN TO ME.

I laughed, and Fernie said, What's that tattoo on your tongue?
He looked closely. He read: PARKING FOR ICE CREAM ONLY.

We employed our tongues on ice cream
As we walked on the beach,
A frightening sight to tourists.

We stripped to our swimming trunks
And dove into the sea—
The tattoos, the stick-on kind, peeled off.
They swayed between waves
And slowly descended under the water,
Where, I like to think, one or two attached themselves
To the fins of two bright but goofy fish.

Internet Café

In Vietnam
We sat in an Internet café
And wrote electronic postcards.

Hi, Mom, I wrote. Wish you were here. Love.

Hey, Dad and Mom, Fernie wrote. We need more money!

I next e-mailed Fernie: Hey, what did you write?

Fernie raised his eyebrows at me from across the café.
He ignored my question.
He tapped and tapped at the keys of his machine.
He wrote: Do you have any sunscreen?

I answered: Yes, it's on my face.

He smiled at me.
He tapped and tapped at the keys of his machine again.
He wrote: Do you have any chewing gum?

I answered: Yes, it's in my mouth.

We left the Internet café.
We took a ride in a motorized rickshaw
And bumped along a road to a store
For more sunscreen and chewing gum,
Plus a squirt gun for each of us.

We had learned this about ourselves.

When we were thirsty, we were thirsty together, at the same time.

We would shoot soda-filled squirt guns into our mouths

That were always opening and closing,

Always perfuming the air with sweet talk.

Even in sleep, we rolled on our cots

And had something to say.

Mexican Food in Taiwan

In Taiwan
Fernie and me rode an elevator up the tallest building
In Asia. We stepped outside—
All the wind in the world was up there.

I laughed. The wind parted Fernie's hair a hundred different ways,
And made my blue chewing gum fly out of my mouth.

Bright me, I said, Let's get some Mexican food for lunch.
When Fernie started to say, But dude, we're in Taiwan,
His blue chewing gum flew from his mouth.

I laughed, but nothing else flew from my mouth.

But Mexican food sounds good, Fernie said.
He described an enchilada special with lots of red, red sauce.
With beans and rice, Fernie crowed.
And guacamole dip, I added, plus a stack of tortillas.

I pointed into the distance.
Me, with my eyes narrowed in the wind, I said, Mexico is over there.
And I swore that I could see a little bit of California.

We talked about Mexican food among Chinese and Japanese tourists.
Then we went down and looked all
Over Taiwan for a Mexican restaurant.

No luck for us.
The only thing we found was blue chewing gum,
Stuck to the bottoms of our shoes.

Fanfare in Mongolia

Thunder, the fingers of lightning,
Clouds like clanging anvils.

Single drop of rain.

American School in India

For fun we visited the school.
We picked up where we left off,
In the back row next to the window,
Where we could make out two boys on the monkey bars—
That was us back at home.

When the teacher wrote on the board,

Solve for x:
$$0 = x^2 - 16x + 64$$

I looked at Fernie, who was using the fingers of one hand
     to do his math.
Me, I snickered at my backward friend.
I was far more advanced—
I was using two hands and the toes on my left foot,
Same toes I would count on, if I had to, to keep myself
Swinging smartly on the monkey bars.

Answer: $x = 8$

The Source of the Nile

We were on an African mountain, a snowy one, tall as the heavens.
We two stood admiring the beauty
Of the planet, though we frowned at some
Litter found below.

We were moved to poetry.

Fernie cried, O Westward Sky.
Not to be outdone, I cried, O Eastward Sky
And Southern Sky.

Fernie made a face at me.
He cried, O Southeastern Sky, O Northern Sky.
Not to be outdone,
I called, O All Directions
And you, too, Stars and Moon.

The stars were beginning to appear,
Along with the moon, our guide called The Bald One.

Fernie and me laughed.
We couldn't compete with nature.
Fernie then uncapped his bottled water.
As he chugged and chugged,
Some rolled down his chin and hit the ground.

The water magically rolled away.
In the early dusk we followed this little stream

Until—wow, what a roar!—the liquid
That touched Fernie's dirty chin and throat
Joined the great river that we—great explorers
On a budget—later discovered was the Nile.

Homesickness

Fernie took picture after picture,
His thumb just over the top part of the lens.

Here were tired legs at the Great Wall of China,
Here was some more of my legs in Thailand.

Here were my legs and some of my hand—
I was holding at my side a piece of sugarcane from Laos.

Here were my knees in Fiji,
Here were my snow-tipped shoes in Nepal.

Look what you've done! I meant to scold,
But I could see that he liked the image of his thumb,

And his real thumb, too.
At night it sometimes plugged his mouth
As he—poor guy!—sobbed in his dreams about faraway home.

Drama

Fernie stepped one too many steps
And found himself in Zambian mud.

Quicksand! Fernie cried, and spilled a lukewarm tear.

Me, I cried, Oh, the misfortune! Oh, the cruelty of stars!
I imagined him slowly sinking
Until what remained was only his hair,
A dirty mop on which a mynah bird would settle
And squawk.

Fernie struggled in mud.
Oh, how he played it up—his foot deep in regular mud
That he pretended was quicksand.
He pulled and pulled on his foot.
His tears turned to sweat.
His face purpled.
Boy, he was a good actor.

Me, I circled my friend.

Does it hurt? I asked, poking a finger at his big toe.

I, then, too, felt the tug of quicksand.

Oh! I cried. Oh! Oh!

We giggled, but not much,

Because suddenly it began to rain.

The earth softened. We began to sink into a mush

Of wet, wet earth that suddenly swelled with snakes and toads,

Insects with legs as tall as our own.

We were ankle-deep, then knee-deep, then waist-deep.

By chance a monkey fell from the tree like fruit

And began to tickle our underarms.

We popped into the air and gripped a tree limb—saved!

We hugged our new friend,

Our hero with his breakfast between his teeth!

We were at a resort, by the way.

We limped off to the hotel's restaurant,

Where on the terrace ordered, in honor of our chimp friend,

Banana milk shakes thick as bubbling mud.

The Things We Hear When We're Lost

The Molopo River was so slow, we outswam its currents,
But suddenly our toes were like propellers—
A pair of crocodiles were tagging behind us.

Their eyes were on the surface,
Their teeth were shiny as mirrors,
And each tooth held the reflection of our wet faces.
They were hungry for us, and we were hungry for life.
Fernie and me swam to the shore.

That was close, huh? I said,
And undid the blow-up swan from my waist.
Fernie stepped out of his blow-up dragon.

We were lost.
Nightfall was coming fast
When a chimp sneaked up from behind and shouted
Eeyupanhanhanhan in my left ear.

I jumped.

What was that? Fernie cried.
He stepped back into his blow-up dragon
And was ready to brave the river again.

I told him,
Someone just screamed *Eeyupanhanhanhan* in my left ear.

The neck of the blow-up dragon drooped.
Fernie looked confused.

I tried again.
I told him that someone screamed, *Eeyupanhanhanhan.*

Fernie scratched his chin.
You sure it wasn't *Uuyupanhanhanhan?*

No, no, I told him. It was *Eeyupanhanhanhan,*
And hitched the blow-up swan around my waist—
I was going to return to the river if I had to.

I shivered.
I boxed mosquitoes from my face.
While we were talking about the dangers of the jungle,
Plus the soggy postcards in our pockets,
I felt the blow-up swan thicken and grow around my waist.
I looked down, only a little scared,
At the chimp who was blasting air into my water toy.
He smiled, all teeth, in the dark.
He jumped up and down
And finished with a blast of *Uuyupanhanhanhan.*

Fernie was right after all, more chimp than me.

Safari

In Kenya
Fernie raised his camera
And snapped a picture of a lion yawning.

I yawned, but Fernie didn't bother with me.
He took a picture of an elephant, also yawning.

No fair, I cried,
And mounted the elephant
And urged him next to the lion, a lazy one in grass,
A friend to bugs that had set up camp in his mane.

Then a rhino joined us, openmouthed,
And a viper that was tall as a sapling.

At the count of one, two, three,
This whole tribe of animals and me yawned for the camera.

Then we relaxed our jaws slowly,
Each of us watching the others—
No telling when a closing mouth turns into a bite.

The Lost Camel of Aswan

Fernie and me were sliding down a sand dune on cardboard,
And would have done it a thousand times more
Except a camel, lost perhaps,
Came to chew its cud and wonder at the sand between
   our front teeth.
Its eyelashes were long, its eyes the color of coffee.
A rope hung from its bridle.

Fernie looked at me, and I looked at him—
In seconds we were on the back of the two-humped camel.

Me, I asked: I wonder how much water these things hold?
I stroked the hump.

About three glasses, Fernie answered.

I rapped the hump with a knuckle.
Its sound as hollow as an empty canteen.
I was suddenly thirsty myself, me, riding under the sun's fiery ring.

We rode up one dune and another
Until Fernie remarked, Do you think we're lost?

The camel had been lost,
And, I guess, we were lost with him.
Yes, I answered, but at least we're together.

We rode another hour.
I'm thirsty, I muttered.

Fernie muttered the same,

Though he added he wouldn't have minded a hamburger

To go along with the drink.

It was then a mirage of sodas and milk shakes appeared,

French fries, too, a taco dripping hot sauce.

And what was that? A bucket of fried chicken?

We licked our lips,

And the camel also licked its lips.

Our friend with two humps seemed to see the mirage as well.

He began to trot, then run,

We two on board tossed about.

But oh, how we hung on,

For the mirage grew to include a swimming pool,

Buckets and buckets of sodas,

Pitchers of lemonade and passion fruit,

Boxes of juice, wax candies that we could chew

And enjoy a syrupy squirt.

We three ran for our lives,

The invisible humps on our backs rising like mountains!

Our eyelashes growing thick as mops!

(This all occurred one regular morning in the Sahara,

To us two boys with cardboard surfboards and sand between
    our teeth.

Now let Fernie tell you about the leopard after lunch . . .)

Lazy Boys

We felt worldly.
Fernie and me swung in a hammock in Greece.
Our shoes were off. Our toes throbbed.
All day we walked up a mountain
And walked down.

We were spoiled with bread and cheese,
Olives and mint leaves that you chew like gum.
To the accordion music from the street
Our toes danced for us.

We were lazy.
Even the breeze rocked our hammock
Without effort.

Touring Russia on Bikes

We put on a Cossack's furry hat
And rode squeaky bicycles.

We were invading Moscow, sort of.
We rode our bikes to St. Peter's Square
And then dropped the bikes to watch
Two pigeons kiss, sort of.

On closer look
I saw that the pigeons were sharing a bagel.

That's cool, Fernie said,
And the two of us walked our horses,
I mean bikes, into a park
Where a man in the smallest chair in the world
Was doing a magic trick before three squirrels.
The coin in his palm disappeared,
Then, seconds later, fell from his ear. He twirled the coin
And let it do backflips over his knuckles.

We applauded.
The squirrels moved on.
Boys, the magician said, give me two coins.

We plunged our hands into our pockets
And brought out a coin each.
He took them, this old man
In the smallest chair in the world.

He breathed on them, shined and gave them new life.
He brought them to his eyes
And then—*presto!*—they were gone.

We gave him more coins.
We waited for the coins to reappear,
But the magician just smiled at us until the smile faded
In the late afternoon, along with the smallest chair
In the world, then he himself.

That's freaky, Fernie said. He's, like, gone!
Me, I had no power of speech,
Only a lower lip that hung open like a sack.

We were tricked!
We got back onto our bikes.
With the coin-bright sun behind us,
We could see our meager shadows
In front of us. Our Cossack hats were tall,
But on the ancient and crooked streets
Of Moscow, our shoulders were defeated.

Off the Aegean Coast

The captain squawked on the intercom, Dress for dinner.

I looked at Fernie, and Fernie looked at me.
Dress for dinner?

We went down to our room, next to the engine room
With its pistons like elephant legs
Going slowly up and down.

We opened up our suitcases—skateboards on their backs,
An empty bag of sunflower seeds,
Poker chips that we pressed to our eyes
When we played Blind Man's Bluff.

Dinner at seven o'clock, the intercom said in our room.

I bit a fingernail, and Fernie rolled a wheel of his skateboard.
We should have packed better, I said,
And Fernie stopped the wheel of our misfortune
And sighed.

We entered the dining room dressed for dinner.
For the way we ate, so messy, so messy,
The soup like a tidal wave in our bowls . . .
We entered wrapped in tablecloths.

Later, in bed, licking our knuckles was a moonlight treat.

Late Snack in Sicily

Fernie was at one end of a salami sausage
And I was at the other.

At first Fernie nibbled slowly
And I followed along,

That is, until he sneakily sped up.
My own teeth sped up,

And he sped, a little bit faster.
What could I do but get my teeth going

Until we, little pigs, snuffled and grunted
At the honker we honored.

Another Kind of Spanish Armada

Fernie peels a Valencia orange and sets the twelve slices,
His armada, on a wooden table in Madrid.

Me, on my knees at the end,
I slowly pull the tablecloth toward me—
Each of the slices falls into my mouth,
A crushing defeat.

Liechtenstein

In a tiny country with a long name,
Fernie and me held hands, stretched, and touched the borders.

Window-Shopping in Lucerne

The cheese in Switzerland had holes,
Lots of holes, and caused Fernie in his new Tyrolean hat
To think that he was in such a poor country.

Holes in the cheese.
He thought of his socks back at home,
In the same condition, and stinky as cheese.

In Paris

Fernie set up an easel by the River Seine,
And I set up mine.

I smacked my brushes against the canvas,
And used mostly red, white, and blue to draw Fernie,
Our American boy.

Fernie attracted tourists.
Me, I attracted three pigeons,
Who nibbled on dropped croissants
And warbled their approval.
One settled on my shoulder, another on my shoe.
The last poked at my artist's palette.

What a clever bird, I told myself,
And left my easel to stroll to the end of the bridge—
While a man squeezed music from an accordion,
Two girls were making a play out of peanut shells
They had fit onto their fingertips
And were telling a story about a family who lived on . . . peanuts.
I felt excited! Moments before, I'd wanted to paint,
But now I was committed
To being a peanut shell—I mean an actor.

When I returned,
The pigeon was poking its paint-filled beak at the canvas.

I stepped back.

I adjusted my beret

And tightened my scarf around my neck like a snake.

I studied the drawing of Fernie with a nose like a beak.

In my actor's voice, I cried, O Picasso of All Pigeons,

O Renoir of the Air, O Chagall of the Telephone Wire in Rain!

The pigeons, in the peanut gallery behind me,

Fanned their wings in applause.

The *Mona Lisa*

The tour guide said, Her famous smile is worth 187 million euros.
We were wowed, Fernie and me,
And left the tour, smiling.

Back in our hotel I practiced the smile in the mirror.
How much? I asked Fernie.
I smiled all the way to the tops of my pink gums.

Six euros, Fernie said.
What? I said angrily.

Seven euros, then, Fernie said, nearly laughing.
I had to laugh, too. We were low on money, so far from home.
I hoped I could sell my smile to an artist.

Once again I smiled all the way to the tops of my pink gums,
And squinted my left eye, made my right eye really big.

Fernie held his stomach, sick,
And reached into his pocket for eight euros—tops, he said.

With that,
I treated my friend to a fresh baguette
And a single sardine,
A little joker fish who was smiling as big as he could!

Educational Opportunity

In an English tourist shop,
Fernie pulled on a Queen's College of Oxford University sweatshirt,
Then sweatshirts of Lincoln College and St. Hugh's College,
Also of Oxford. He bought a Cambridge sweatshirt
And slipped that one on, too. Plus a sweatshirt from
The London School of Economics,
And Fernie couldn't forget the University of Bristol
And the University of St. Andrew's, Scotland's oldest,
Built in a time when the daddy of the thatched house created fire
By knocking rocks together. Fernie patted his belly
And lectured the mirror where he stood: Boy, I'm fat!

A scholar, Fernie tottered around London.
He never knew that education was such sweaty work.

Scottish Attire

Fernie put on a little muscle
When he squeezed a bagpipe in the Highlands.

Then we rolled boulders up a hill—
Another Scottish pastime, we were told.

Man, that's a lot of work, Fernie said,
And soaped his exhausted fingers in a basin.

I looked out our hotel window.
Sheep were gathering in the meadow.
Darkness was closing like a fist.
I was moved. I cried, O Beautiful Scotland!

We slipped into kilts and I warned Fernie, You better not tell!
He said, And you better not tell, either!

So in our plaid kilts we came downstairs.
Me, I said cheerio to the woman behind the desk,
A woman wearing pants and smoking a pipe.

Fernie punched me in the arm.
They don't say *cheerio* here—that's in England.

Righto, I answered,
And Fernie said, They don't say that here, either!

Tallyho, I called to Fernie as we reached the large wooden door
Where a collie slept, one tender paw over the other.

Or that word, either! Fernie cried.

I was confused.
In the early dark we walked outside
And the wind lifted our skirts—
Bashful us, under that length of tartan,
We were wearing our jeans rolled up to our knees.

The Influence of Penguins

In Patagonia we had all the ice we liked,
Since we were lost on an iceberg.

I'm freezing, Fernie said.
Be brave, I cried, chattering through my teeth.
We passed another iceberg with a convention
Of penguins, all dressed up,
Slapping their tiny wings at their sides.
They were throwing back fish two at a time.

The penguins, one after another, dipped into the water
And climbed up onto our iceberg.
They circled us. They flapped their tiny wings,
Stirring up body heat.

We were saved! We were loved by penguins!
During our five days near the South Pole
We walked around in short steps, arms flapping at our side,
Raw fish our favorite food and tuxedoes our daily wear.

Buenos Aires

We checked into a fancy hotel
To a suite of rooms with a chandelier that could have lit up
 a football stadium.
Immediately Fernie and me looked in the refrigerator—
Sodas and ice cream, plus candy bars
And ropes of red licorice long enough to scale down the side
Of our hotel.

We drank and ate, then jumped on the bed.
Fernie got on the telephone. Room service, my good man, he said,
And ordered a second bed, along with more to eat,
And a video camera. We had plans, big ones,
We, the Exercise Kings of Argentina—
Two boys jumping endlessly
On the human rocket fuel called sugar.

The world could use one more foolproof diet plan.

The Road Not Taken . . . in Peru

When Fernie and me came to a fork in the road,
I said, Hey, let's go this way.
Fernie shook his head. Nah, let's head this way—
I can see some llamas over there.

I looked. I said, Nah, we've already seen llamas.
Yeah, but not these ones, Fernie argued.

So Fernie took one road, and I took another.
Five weeks on our world trip, and maybe we had seen too much
Of each other.

I walked up my road, Fernie his,
And I could see him because my road was only a few feet away,
Close enough that I could reach out and touch his shoulder.

We trekked for a mile, and then another mile—
Fernie got to see his llamas and I got to stop and pet a turtle
In my road. Then things got scary—
We were momentarily separated by bushes,
A single fallen tree,
And boulders the color and shape of elephants.

When our roads converged,
We jumped into each other's arms,
And I said, after a hundred hugs,
Boy, you should have seen the turtle in my road!

Fernie became dreamy.
We retraced our steps. He went down mine, me his,
And we found ourselves wiser from traveling both roads.

How I Got to Walk Down
Six Thousand Feet Barefoot

We climbed the heights of Machu Picchu
And at the top of the world
We rested to view the ruins.

Fernie said, The air is thin.
I looked around.
What do you mean?

He said he didn't know,
But had read it in a book—
Something about air getting thin the higher you go up.

I took off my shoes and pounded out sand and rock.
I didn't understand it, either, the thin-air thing.

Then Fernie took off his shoes.
He pounded out rock and sand and a Y-shaped twig.

We stood up.
O Beautiful World, I cried.
O Majestic Purple Sun, Fernie cried on his tiptoes.
I looked at Fernie. Purple sun?

Poetry, Fernie said, still on his tiptoes. Liberty of language, buddy boy.
Well, me, I didn't know about poetry or thin air,
Or gravity, either, because the next second
By accident I kicked our shoes down the heights of Machu Picchu.

See what you've done? Fernie cried.

I'm sorry, I said and, to get on his good side, agreed with his poetry.

I proclaimed to the heavens, O Purple Sun! O Sun of Unusual Color!

What was the big deal?

Fernie climbed on my back.

I carried him down those heights like a llama,

High in the great ruins and, with my lungs working for breath,

Mighty thin air!

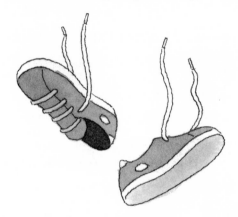

Happiness

We took a watermelon down to the Amazon River

And cracked it open on a rock.

We ate at the shore.

Full, we lay in the grass.

Twilight, then darkness. The sound of water flowing.

Crickets, the swoop of bats,

And the moon shepherding a flock of stars

To a new day.

Regret Near the Border of Bolivia and Brazil

Fernie tossed a stone into the Amazon River
And felt like tossing himself next—
He had forgotten to feed his goldfish before he left home!

Woe is me, Fernie bawled.
My poor goldfish!

(Birds the color of a box of crayons faded in the trees,
Fruit the world had never tried fell like rocks,
And in shadows a puma sat licking the bottoms of its paws.)

Feeling bad, Fernie tested the river's quickly moving water
With a big toe. A piranha raised its head
From the surface, hungry for flesh. Fernie pulled it back
And sat on the river's edge to apologize to his big toe,
The instrument that kicked a field goal to break a 79–79 tie
    in the fourth quarter—
How could he be so mean to his own flesh!

Poor Goldie, Fernie bawled even louder
As he envisioned a mere skeleton
On the pebbled bottom of the fishbowl. Behind closed eyes,
He saw the last bubble of breath rise and snap on the surface.

Fernie was crying
When I approached, eating a mango.
I handed him a letter from home—
His tears blurred the address on the envelope,
But he could see through his tears that everything was super
At home. His baby brother, now a big boy,
Was feeding his goldfish.

Why were you crying? I asked.

He explained his sorrow.
I stopped eating my mango for a second.
Thoughtless me, I asked, Who's feeding your cat, then?

Fernie blinked, frowned,
And buried his face in his hands.
Ah, my poor cat! Fernie cried.

Bad boy me, I thought for a quarter of a quarter of a second,
Maybe the cat could eat the goldfish!

Paraguay Makes Great Candles

Fernie and me rode the rapids of the mighty Orinoco River
And, naked on the shore,
Soaped ourselves until we were white with suds.
We resembled sheep. We attracted two sheep,
Who nudged us with their furry heads.
Poor things, they got soap in their eyes!

We wiped their eyes.
Oh, how the day was great!

Nighttime. Cool wind blew off the river.

We crawled into our tent on the shore.

Fernie told me a spooky story about a boy with chicken legs,

And I told a story about a girl with chicken legs.

We scared ourselves.

When our flashlight went dead, we brought out a candle.

Fernie passed his hand over the candle

And said, That didn't hurt.

I passed my hand over the candle, too, only closer.

Then Fernie passed his over, even closer.

That didn't hurt, either, he claimed.

I passed my hand, almost touching the wick.

Fernie passed his hand over the wick, touching it.

Not to be outdone, I pressed my thumb into the wick.

Fernie whistled, impressed by my bravery.

The sheep baaed outside our tent.

Hey, he suggested,

Now let's do it with the candle burning.

Calling Home From Jamaica

Fernie spent a day running from mosquitoes,
And suddenly lonely for a voice
Other than mine, he called home.
He got his answering machine:
Hello, this is Fearless Fernie. I'll be away
For a while. You can leave a message if you're calling
About the bicycle—it's still for sale.
If you're calling about the rowboat,
That's already been sold—you should
Have called earlier. If you're calling about mowing a lawn,
Contact my friend Jason at 849-0282—he'll be taking
Over my practice while I'm gone. If it's you, Robert,
Sorry I didn't have time to return your CDs
Before I left on my world trip.

Fernie smiled and hung up.
He made a face at the faceless mosquitoes
Trying to get through the netting over his bed.
In love with his voice, he pressed redial:
Hello, this is Fearless Fernie. I'll be away . . .

The Romantics

In Pakistan
Fernie bought a small pillow
And carried it with him.
How the chickens of Ecuador clucked at the pillow,
For it was filled with the feathers of their ancestors—
They say that chickens originated in Asia.

And it was while we were on our trip Fernie started liking girls.
Fernie liked a girl in Norway,
He liked two in Tunisia.

Then in Guatemala
Fernie slept on the pillow by Lake Atitlán.
Shipment after shipment of small waves arrived at the shore.
Fernie was in love. I could tell by his smile, his kicking feet.
When I peeled back his eyelids,
I could see in his dream all the girls he liked.

Me, I wasn't envious,
For I was still in love with the sweets of the world.
Near sleep, I could read the menu on the inside of my eyelids.

O Double-Dark Chocolate of Switzerland,
O Gelato of Italy, O Truffles of France,
O Mango Lassi of India on another hot day!

Professional Goals

Fernie and me tried surfing in Mazatlán
And then lay on a towel on the beach,
Where we lit a campfire.

While waves crashed and the sun burned on the sea's horizon,
We ate fish tacos.

We were coming to the end of our trip.
I asked Fernie, What do you want to be when you grow up?

Fernie took off his sunglasses, ignored me.
Wow, he said, it's nighttime.

I looked around.
Yeah, of course it's nighttime.

The moon was now up, the stars squeezing their icy light.

I ate another fish taco.
I chewed and cleared my throat
And repeated myself. What do you want to be?

A forest fire fighter, he answered, then clicked the sunglasses
Between the tops and bottoms of his teeth.
No, a fire fighter in a movie.
No, a fire fighter in a TV comedy.
No, a fire fighter in a play that takes place on a beach.

Fernie gazed sleepily at the campfire.
He was such a lazy one. With a toe
He splashed some sand on the campfire, his one effort
Of fighting fire.

Higher Sights

The bus between Oaxaca and Mexico City broke down.
That was okay with us. We got out, stretched.
Fernie walked away to admire a tree
Bearded with monarch butterflies.

Alone, I raised my binoculars, adjusted the sight,
And made out a pitted moon rock. The landscape was destroyed,
Useless. My goodness! I cried, and was never so amazed
By the sudden twitching of that lunar rock.
I was scared by the appearance of a long-necked dinosaur
Entering a cave. Chills rode the smooth
Roads of my arms and gathered
Near my neck. I let the binoculars fall.

What did I have my sights on? A close-up
Of Fernie picking his nose by the fanning wings
Of princely butterflies.

Last Stop Outside of Tucson, Arizona

Fernie and me were still best friends,
And on the last day of our trip
We were out of money.

We had a spotted banana, though,
That we cut so thin, we could see through each slice.

We licked our sweetened thumbs
And used them to hitchhike home—
By chance a sports car stopped,
Though we were wearing our African masks,
Our Mexican sandals, our Scottish kilts,
Our Italian scarf, our French berets with a smudge of paint,
And our sweatshirts from the major English universities.

And by chance
The driver was Mrs. Podsakoff, our third-grade teacher!
She said, Wipe your noses!
We took off our masks and did what we were told,
Then climbed into her sports car.
It was no big deal that we were bringing home a llama
Loaded down with 348 rolls of undeveloped film
And a jar of Amazonian water that could cure hiccups,
Another llama weighed down with baskets from Costa Rica,
A rug from Tibet, a kite from China,
And bags of Egyptian popcorn to toss freely on our arrival—
Our neighborly pigeons were waiting for us.

We were wiser, we were darker,

We were coming home, bringing the world inside us.

Mrs. Podsakoff, a teacher who never let up, quizzed us.

What's the capital of Kenya? *Nairobi.*

The capital of Norway? *Oslo.*

The major export of Venezuela? *Oil.*

The native language of Peru? *Quechuan.*

The ruins of Tikal are in what country? *Guatemala.*

The first explorers to round the Cape of Good Hope?

I looked at Fernie, and Fernie looked at me. *Us?*

Wrong, you two! Mrs. Podsakoff scolded us lightly,

But patted our heads lightly. You were good boys,

She said, and we sat up, all smiles. I'm proud of you!

I always knew you two would go far!

California Geography

Gilroy has the garlic,
Watsonville the strawberry of a good-bye kiss.
Los Banos parades the tomato,
That thick red transfusion in a ketchup bottle.

The watermelon is plunged into ice in Kingsburg,
And an almond shell is tossed over a shoulder in Del Rey.
Flies pester an ear of corn in Sacramento.
Bees circle the sweet cantaloupe rind in Huron,
Valley town the summer moon washes clean.

The chili stings the pickers outside of Fresno,
The onions sob in Kerman,
And the grapes hang in the air under a Selma arbor.
The citizens march for their fruits, their veggies.
Let them have the stains at the corners of their mouths.

Salinas speaks up for the artichoke,
Half Moon Bay for the broccoli and boulders of pumpkin.
Knee-deep in berry vines, deer busy themselves
West of Highway One.

But what city claims the pinto bean,
Little trouper boiling in a pot on the back burner?
Stir this broth and spank a frijol
When it rises to the surface,
Frijol with no city, no parade.
It's like us, Fernie and me,
Commoners fallen absently
Onto the kitchen floor and left unnoticed,

Like us, like us, steaming.